Sue Bentley

Magic Puppy

Sunshine Shimmers

Illustrated by Angela Swan

PUFFIN

To Champion – wonderful and steadfast

PUFFIN BOOKS

Published by the Penguin Group
Penguin Books Ltd, 80 Strand, London WC2R 0RL, England
Penguin Group (USA) Inc., 375 Hudson Street, New York, New York 10014, USA
Penguin Group (Canada), 90 Eglinton Avenue East, Suite 700, Toronto, Ontario, Canada M4P 2Y3
(a division of Pearson Penguin Canada Inc.)
Penguin Ireland, 25 St Stephen's Green, Dublin 2, Ireland (a division of Penguin Books Ltd)
Penguin Group (Australia), 250 Camberwell Road, Camberwell, Victoria 3124, Australia
(a division of Pearson Australia Group Pty Ltd)
Penguin Books India Pvt Ltd, 11 Community Centre, Panchsheel Park, New Delhi – 110 017, India
Penguin Group (NZ), 67 Apollo Drive, Rosedale, North Shore 0632, New Zealand
(a division of Pearson New Zealand Ltd)
Penguin Books (South Africa) (Pty) Ltd, 24 Sturdee Avenue, Rosebank,
Johannesburg 2196, South Africa

Penguin Books Ltd, Registered Offices: 80 Strand, London WC2R 0RL, England

puffinbooks.com

First published 2009
4

Text copyright © Sue Bentley, 2009
Illustrations copyright © Angela Swan, 2009
All rights reserved

The moral right of the author and illustrator has been asserted

Set in Bembo
Made and printed in England by Clays Ltd, St Ives plc

British Library Cataloguing in Publication Data
A CIP catalogue record for this book is available from the British Library

ISBN: 978–0–141–32476–0

Mixed Sources
Product group from well-managed
forests and other controlled sources
www.fsc.org Cert no. SA-COC-1592
© 1996 Forest Stewardship Council

Penguin Books is committed to a sustainable future
for our business, our readers and our planet.
The book in your hands is made from paper
certified by the Forest Stewardship Council.

Prologue

The young silver-grey wolf raised his
head and looked up at the mountain
tops, which were veiled by mist. Storm
took a deep breath. It felt good to be
back. He wondered where his mother
might be hiding.

Suddenly a terrifying howl shattered
the silence.

'Shadow!' Storm gasped, realizing that

the fierce lone wolf who had attacked his Moon-claw pack and family was very close.

There was a bright flash and a dazzling shower of golden sparks. Where Storm had been standing there now crouched a tiny fluffy ginger-and-black Yorkshire terrier puppy with a pointed face, pricked ears and midnight-blue eyes.

Storm trembled, hoping that his puppy disguise would protect him from the evil Shadow. Keeping his furry belly close to the ground, Storm crept towards a clump of rocks.

As he approached, one of the rocks seemed to move. Storm's tiny heart beat fast as he picked out the shape of a large adult wolf and saw the gleam of familiar bright golden eyes.

The tiny puppy's whole body wriggled and his tail twirled. 'Mother!' Storm yapped with relief. With a whimper of greeting he leapt forward and began licking Canista's mouth and nose.

'I am glad you are safe and well, my son, but you have returned at a dangerous time,' Canista said in a warm velvety growl. She nuzzled her disguised cub's little ginger-and-black face, but then gave a sharp wince of pain.

'Let me help you!' Storm blew out a gentle stream of tiny gold sparks, which swirled round a nasty bite on Canista's leg for a few seconds and then disappeared.

'Thank you, Storm. The pain is easing. But there isn't time now for you to help me recover all my powers as well. You must go — Shadow is very close,' Canista rumbled softly.

Sadness rippled through Storm's tiny puppy body as he thought of his father and litter brothers and the once proud Moon-claw wolves, now gone or scattered. His midnight-blue eyes flashed with anger. 'One day I will stand beside you and face Shadow and force him to leave our lands forever!'

Canista nodded proudly. 'And then the others will accept you as their leader and the Moon-claw pack will run together again. But until then you must use this disguise and hide in the other world. Return when you are wiser and your magic is stronger.'

Another fierce howl split the air.

The sound of iron-hard paws was like thunder on the hillside. Powerful claws scrabbled at the rocks, close to where Storm and his mother hid. 'I know you are here! Let us finish this!' Shadow growled coldly.

'Go now, Storm! Save yourself!' Canista urged.

Bright gold sparks ignited in the tiny puppy's ginger-and-black fur. Storm whined softly as he felt the power gathering inside him. Golden light pooled brightly around him. And grew brighter . . .

Chapter
ONE

Della Walton sighed as she sat next to her mum in the busy airport at Valencia.

'Cheer up, love,' her mum said. 'I'm sure our luggage will turn up. Your dad's gone to find someone who can help to track it down.'

'I know. But it's not just that,' Della said dejectedly, thinking about Chloe, who was meant to have come with them on their Spanish holiday. But at the last minute her younger cousin had decided that she'd miss her parents too much and was staying at home. Della was certain that the holiday wasn't going to be half as much fun without Chloe to play with.

'I know you're disappointed about your cousin, but I'm sure you'll meet some new friends,' her mum said.

Della hoped so. She tried to smile, for her mum's sake, but she couldn't make herself cheer up. It felt like a big black cloud was hanging over her head.

She saw her dad weaving towards them through the crowds of people. 'Well, that was a waste of time,' he said crossly. 'A whole lot of luggage has gone astray and no one has any idea where it is. We're to go on to the villa and the airport staff will get in touch when ours turns up. I've left them our contact details.'

'Oh, dear. Well, I suppose we'd better pick up the car and get going,' Mrs Walton said in her calm, practical way. 'It's a good thing we've got our money and all the important stuff.'

Della trudged after her mum and dad as they stepped outside the airport terminal. Bright sunshine shone down on beds of palm trees and giant cacti.

They picked up their car and soon joined the busy traffic on the motorway.

Della stared gloomily out of the window at the towns they passed, baking in the sun, and the lines of cars and huge

lorries. After about twenty minutes the traffic thinned out and the scenery was replaced by shady groves of olive and orange trees and green fields with low farmhouses.

Overhead, the sky was a clear, bright blue. Despite herself, Della gradually felt her spirits starting to lift a bit. She was about to ask if they were there yet, when they turned on to a narrow road that snaked up the side of a hill.

'There's our villa!' Mrs Walton said, pointing.

Della caught a glimpse of white walls and a red-tiled roof through the trees. Maybe things would get better once they got there. She began looking forward to a long cool drink as she relaxed and splashed around in the pool.

But as their car drew to a halt outside the villa Della caught her breath. Metal shutters covered all the windows, the lawn was long and straggly and the pool was a sludgy greenish colour.

'You must have made a mistake, Dad! This is the wrong place!' she exclaimed. There was no way she was swimming in that pool!

Scratching his head, her dad checked the address. 'No. This is it, all right. I don't understand what's gone wrong. The owner lives in a farm just a few metres further on.' He turned to his wife. 'Why don't you and Della relax in the shade while I go and have a word with her?'

Mrs Walton nodded. 'Good idea.' She got out of the car and then sank on to a wooden bench beneath a tree.

'I'm going to have a look around,'
Della decided, wandering off down a
winding path past some flower beds.
'First I'm left with no one to play with
and now the villa's a dump. This holiday's
one giant disaster,' she grumbled, starting
to wish that she'd stayed at home too. At
least then she and Chloe could have had
fun together.

She had just reached some palm trees
when there was a dazzling flash of bright
light that lit up the white-painted garden
wall.

'Oh!' Della blinked, blinded for a
moment. She looked up, expecting to
see dark clouds gathering after what she
thought was a flash of lightning. But it
was still calm and sunny.

Feeling puzzled, Della looked back at

the trees and saw a tiny cute puppy with
ginger-and-black fur, a pointed face
and huge midnight-blue eyes. Hundreds
of tiny sparkles, like miniature fireflies,
gleamed in its fluffy coat.

   She frowned. What was a puppy
doing here with the villa closed up and
deserted? Maybe its owners had left it

behind when they left. 'You poor little thing. Are you all alone?' she murmured wonderingly.

The puppy stood up and shook itself. 'Yes, I am. I have come from far away. Can you help me?' it woofed.

Chapter
TWO

Della stared down at the puppy in
surprise. The Spanish heat must have
made her feel funny – she'd just imagined
that it had spoken to her!

She fanned herself with her hands to
cool down a little. The puppy was so cute,
but her mum had told her it was best not
to touch animals abroad. So she sat down
on one of the low walls a little way away.

'I suppose you might belong to someone at the farm. Or maybe you're a stray,' she said to herself.

'I do not belong to anyone,' the puppy woofed.

Della's eyes widened with shock. She almost toppled back off the wall on to her behind.

'Y-you r-really can t-talk!' she stammered, straightening up.

The puppy pricked his tiny ears. 'All the wolves in my world can talk. My

name is Storm of the Moon-claw pack. What is yours?' it woofed again.

Della gulped. Talking dogs did not just appear to ordinary girls in real life, except in fairy stories. But this puppy had and it was blinking up at her expectantly with the brightest eyes she had ever seen, waiting for her answer.

'I'm D-Della Walton,' she found herself replying.

'I am honoured to meet you, Della.' The puppy bowed his little head. 'Where is this place?' Despite his tiny size, Della noticed that Storm seemed strangely unafraid of her.

'It's a villa in Spain. I'm here on holiday with my parents. At least, we're supposed to be. So far, everything's gone wrong,' she said. She frowned and looked round nervously. 'Did . . . did you just say something about a wolf pack?'

Storm nodded proudly. 'My mother and father led our Moon-claw pack. But an evil lone wolf attacked us. He is called Shadow. My father and litter brothers were killed and my mother is wounded and in hiding. Shadow wants to be leader, but the others are waiting for me to return. I am here alone in this world.'

'But how can you lead a wolf pack? You're a tiny pup–' Della stopped as Storm held up a tiny fluffy front paw and began backing away.

There was another dazzling bright flash and a burst of gold sparks showered over Della, crackling around her feet on to the grass.

Della rubbed her eyes, and when she could see again she saw that the tiny ginger-and-black puppy had gone. In its place now stood an amazing young wolf with thick silver-grey fur and glowing midnight-blue eyes.

'Storm?' Della gasped nervously, eyeing the wolf's large teeth and thick neck ruff that glimmered with hundreds of gold sparks like tiny yellow diamonds.

'Yes, Della, it is me,' Storm said in a deep velvety growl. Do not be afraid.'

Before Della could get used to seeing Storm as a handsome silver wolf there was a final gold flash and he appeared again as a cute fluffy ginger-and-black puppy.

'Wow! You really are a wolf. No one would ever know!' she said, bending down again and holding out her hand.

Della decided that it would be fine to stroke a magic puppy.

To her delight, Storm edged closer and brushed her fingers with his damp little nose. His tail wagged nervously and she saw that he was beginning to tremble all over. 'Shadow will know if he finds me. Will you help me to hide?'

Della's heart went out to the helpless little puppy. 'Of course I will . . .' She tailed off as she realized that she didn't know what was going to happen about the villa. 'Except that I'm not sure where we'll be staying now. I'd love to take you with me, but I don't think Mum will be that keen on me adopting a stray. And I don't see how I can smuggle you into our car without anyone noticing,' she said thoughtfully.

'Do not worry. I will use my magic so that only you will be able to see and hear me,' Storm woofed.

'You can make yourself invisible? Wow!' Della said breathlessly. 'No problem then. You can stay with me, wherever we end up!'

'Della! Where are you? Your dad's coming back,' called her mum's voice.

Della looked round. 'Coming!' she

called. She turned back to Storm. 'Can you make yourself invisible now?'

Storm nodded. A cloud of tiny gold sparks glittered in his fluffy fur and then went out. 'It is done.'

As Della began walking back through the garden Storm padded along invisibly beside her. She smiled to herself. When her mum had said that she might meet new friends on this holiday she had never imagined that it would be a magic puppy!

'There's been a mix-up,' Della's dad explained. 'Maria Isola, who lets out the villa, thought we were arriving next week. She's very apologetic and insists that she cooks us all a meal. We can relax at the farm while she and her daughter get the villa ready for us.'

Mrs Walton nodded slowly. 'Well, that's good of her. And it will save us trying to find somewhere to eat out.'

Storm's probably hungry too and ready for a rest after his long journey, Della thought, biting back a grin. She still couldn't quite get used to having the tiny puppy sitting next to her while her mum and dad were completely unaware of him. But as they continued to take no notice of Storm she felt herself beginning to relax.

Mrs Walton ruffled Della's short brown hair. 'Well done on coping with all this so well, honey. I know you were already disappointed about Chloe.'

'I guess it's not all been that bad,' Della said, looking at Storm and smiling to herself.

Her dad grinned. 'That's my girl!'

They decided to walk to the farmhouse as it was so close. 'After all, we haven't got any heavy cases to carry,' Mrs Walton reasoned.

Della felt better for the first time since their plane had landed. It would have been so cool to share her amazing new secret with Chloe, who she knew would have loved Storm, but Della decided that it was even more special to keep it all to herself. She dawdled along and let her mum and dad walk in front, enjoying having Storm scampering along beside her on his short ginger-and-black legs.

Della wondered if she still might meet someone her age to be friends with this holiday. *Then,* she thought wistfully, *this could just turn out to be my best holiday ever!*

Chapter
THREE

The farmhouse and buildings were built round an open-ended courtyard. Soft early evening light cast long shadows across the ground.

'Oh, it's really pretty,' Della said admiringly, glancing at the stone well and red and yellow flowers, which glowed from terracotta pots and window boxes.

A dark-haired woman came out of

a barn and began scattering handfuls of grain for some chickens that were scratching around in the dust. A smile lit up her face when she spotted Della and her parents.

'That's Mrs Isola,' Della's dad said.

'*Hola!*' The Spanish woman greeted them cheerfully. 'Welcome. Come inside. And please call me Maria.' After more apologies about the mix-up Maria made them all cold drinks and then set about making food.

A tall dark-haired girl came into the kitchen. She looked about twelve and was carrying a bucket and cleaning things. Maria introduced her as Carmella, her daughter.

'Hi, I mean, *hola*,' Della said, grinning.

Carmella smiled. 'I am pleased to meet

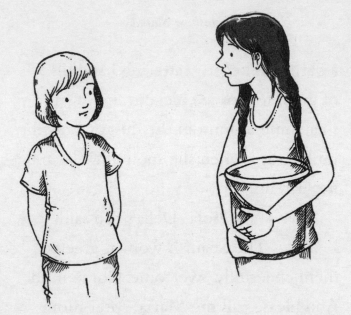

you. I have to make a start on your villa,
but I hope that I will see you later.'

'Me too,' Della said.

Della quickly made sure that no one
was watching her before whispering to
Storm, 'I'm glad that Carmella and her
mum speak good English. I'm not that
great at languages, even though I've been
practising with my Spanish phrase book.'

Storm blinked at her with intelligent

bright eyes. 'What is a phrase book?'

'It's got useful sayings in it, in Spanish, like "How much is this?" and "Where is there a chemist?" But sometimes you can't find the thing you really want to say!'

'I can use my magic to help you to do that,' Storm offered helpfully.

'Really? Wow! Thanks. I'll let you know if I need it,' Della said. Storm was full of surprises. She wondered what else her amazing little friend could do.

Maria soon rustled up a meal of spicy-sausage-and-potato omelette, tomato salad and crusty bread. Della, Storm and her mum and dad sat at an outside table to eat. After making sure they had everything they needed Maria went off to join her daughter in getting the villa ready.

The food was delicious. Storm jumped
up to sit on Della's lap and she was able
to secretly slip bits of food to him. He
gobbled up the omelette and then licked
his chops, seeking out every last tasty
morsel with his little pink tongue.

Della had finished eating and was
stroking Storm's soft fur when suddenly

she felt something hit her lightly on the side of the head. 'Oh!' Puzzled, she looked round, but couldn't see anything.

Her mum and dad were talking and hadn't noticed. A moment later something bounced on to Della's shoulder. This time an unripe olive landed on the grass next to her.

'Wroo-oof?' Storm pricked his ears and sat up straight, before looking towards some nearby bushes.

Della followed the tiny puppy's gaze. She saw the branches move slightly. A girl's face peeped out, framed by the leaves. She had blonde hair and looked about eleven years old. Her eyes were sparkling mischievously.

Della blinked in astonishment. Who was that? She didn't look like part of

Maria's family. She looked again and saw the girl put a finger to her pursed lips before grinning. Della got the message to stay quiet. She nodded, intrigued. The branches shifted again and the girl was hidden from sight.

Storm jumped down and scampered over to investigate. Della heard him barking excitedly and then saw him sniffing round the bushes before running back towards her.

'The girl has gone,' he woofed. 'I saw her run out to the lane outside.'

Della leaned down and pretended to fiddle with her flip-flops so that she could whisper to him. 'I wonder who she was. And how come she's in Maria's garden?'

Storm's midnight-blue eyes widened. 'We could follow her and find out. I can follow her scent trail.'

Della was tempted. The girl could be someone her own age to talk to, but she didn't think her mum and dad would let her go off by herself when she didn't know her way around. 'I'd better not just now,' she decided.

Mr Walton stood up and stretched. 'I'm ready to drop. I wonder how soon we can get into our villa.'

'Why don't we walk back and see how

Maria and Carmella are getting on?' Della suggested, thinking that they might bump into the mystery girl.

'Good idea,' her mum said.

The light was already fading as Della followed them with Storm close at heel. Shadows deepened over the hillside, with its orange and lemon trees and fields stretching into the distance. There was no sign of the girl.

At their villa, the windows and doors were all open. The patio had been swept and a table and chairs set out. The smell of freshly cut grass hung in the air.

Maria met them with a smile. 'Come. I will show you all to your rooms.'

Della, Storm and her mum and dad followed Maria gratefully up the wooden staircase.

Della's room had white walls and beams across the ceiling. There was a single bed and a matching chest and wardrobe of carved dark wood. Her window had shutters instead of curtains.

Storm began nosing round the room, snuffling up all the interesting smells. He finished exploring and jumped up on to the bed. Sighing contentedly, he curled up on the cotton blanket and put his nose between his front paws.

Della stroked her sleepy friend's soft little head. 'You stay there. I'll just pop next door to tell Mum and Dad that I'm having an early night.'

As she returned to her bedroom a minute later, a wave of tiredness washed over her. Storm's little snuffly puppy snores were already floating on the air.

'He's so sweet,' Della whispered to herself as she went to the window. She caught a brief glimpse of another villa through the trees before she closed the shutters and the room was plunged into complete darkness.

Storm's tiny form was gleaming softly on the bed, like a golden nightlight. Della climbed under the cotton sheet and blanket and curled herself around him.

'Night night. Sleep tight,' she

whispered.

'Grr-rrrf.' Storm stirred and opened one sleepy, glowing blue eye and then closed it again.

Chapter
FOUR

'Yay! Our luggage has been found and
Dad's just gone to the airport to pick
it up!' Della told Storm excitedly the
following afternoon. 'I can get my cossie
for a swim in the pool. I was starting to
think that I'd have to spend the whole
holiday in these same jeans and T-shirt.'

Storm's little muzzle wrinkled in a
smile and he wagged his tail.

'It feels like the holiday's starting to get much better now – at last,' Della commented. 'Let's go outside.'

Storm followed Della out to where her mum was sitting reading in the garden beyond the pool. Carmella was just leaving after delivering fresh towels. The older girl smiled at Della and Storm as they walked round the swimming pool.

Della gave her a friendly wave.

Suddenly Storm did a double take and skittered sideways. Della had to swerve to avoid tripping over him. 'Oops. Almost fell over my own feet!' she said for Carmella and her mum's benefit.

Storm stood with his hackles raised, peering down into the murky water. 'Come out and fight! Show yourself!' he challenged, growling.

Della felt a faint tingling sensation
flowing down her spine as tiny sparks
began glinting in Storm's fluffy ginger-
and-black fur.

'What is it? What can you see?' she
asked, forgetting to whisper and then she
noticed that the Spanish girl was looking

at her in puzzlement. 'I mean . . . I can see something in the pool! Something's moving down there!' Della corrected herself hastily.

Carmella smiled. 'That is only the pool robot. It is an underwater cleaner that purifies the water. You will be able to swim in a day or two.'

Della hadn't noticed the ridged plastic tube leading from the power point in the pool house and disappearing into the water. 'Oh, right,' she said, feeling a bit silly but also disappointed that she still wouldn't be able to play in the pool. Della wondered if she and Storm would be having much fun this week.

Carmella smiled kindly at her and carried on walking back towards the farmhouse.

The tingling feeling down Della's back faded as the gold sparks in the tiny puppy's fur went out.

Storm laid back his ears and looked embarrassed. 'I am sorry, Della. I did not mean to make a fuss,' he yapped apologetically.

Della felt a surge of affection for her brave little friend. 'That's OK. You were just trying to protect me, weren't you?'

She wished she could give Storm a cuddle, but she couldn't risk it with her mum so close. 'Any good?' Della asked, nodding towards the book her mum was reading.

Her mum smiled. 'It'll keep. Do you fancy a walk? It'll be a while before your dad gets back.'

'Cool!'

At the mention of a walk, Storm
twirled his tail eagerly. He gambolled
invisibly after Della as she and her mum
set out.

A path at the side of their villa snaked
down the hillside. It was very hot. Lush
creepers covered with pink and purple

blossoms trailed over fences and the sides of buildings.

A large blue butterfly rose from the grass. Storm yapped excitedly as he launched himself at it, but then he tripped over his own paws and collapsed in a furry heap. Jumping to his feet, he shook himself before ambling off to explore a patch of wild flowers.

Della felt a bubble of laughter rising in her chest and quickly turned it into a cough. Sometimes it was hard to believe that Storm was really a magnificent young wolf!

A warm breeze blew towards them, bringing the sound of laughter and splashing from the villa that Della had glimpsed from her bedroom window.

'Anyone want a cold drink?' called a woman's voice.

'It sounds like another English family is staying there,' Mrs Walton said.

'Can we go and say hello?' Della asked eagerly, hoping the family had children.

Her mum went to knock on the door. It was opened by a woman with curly hair and a friendly smile. As Della's mum and the other woman were introducing

themselves, a blonde girl ran out and
came towards Della and Storm. She
looked about eleven years old and was
wearing pink shorts over a striped halter-
neck swimsuit.

Della recognized her at once. It was the
girl who had been hiding in the bushes in
Maria's garden! 'Hi!' she called to her. 'Are
you staying here?'

The girl smiled and nodded. 'This is
our villa. Hey, I know you! You're the girl
I saw yesterday. I was bored, so I sneaked
into Maria's garden and hid in that bush
for a laugh. You should have seen your
face when I was chucking those olives
at you! I'm Honey, Honey Green, by the
way.'

'Hi, I'm Della Walton. I nearly had
kittens when I saw your face looking out

at me!' she said, grinning.

Honey laughed and tossed back her long blonde hair. 'So, where are you staying?'

'In the villa, just up the hill.'

'Great! So we can do stuff together,' Honey said.

Della was delighted. Maybe Honey could be the friend she'd been hoping to make!

'Do you like swimming?' Honey asked.

'Yeah! I love it. But we can't use our pool until it's been cleaned.' Della pulled a face as she explained about the mix-up with their arrival date.

'Oh, what a pain!' Honey said. 'You must be really fed up. I know! Why don't you come and use our pool. Mum and Dad won't mind. You can have a swim

right now . . .'

'Hold your horses, Honey. We're just
about to go out, remember?' Mrs Green
smiled at her daughter and then turned
back to Della. 'But you're welcome any
time, Della. Why don't you come over
tomorrow?'

'Thanks. I'd love to!' Della beamed, looking forward to her first swim and to spending time with Honey.

Della and her mum said their goodbyes and started back to their villa.

'Well, you two girls seemed to be getting on very well,' Mrs Walton commented. 'Honey seems very . . . lively.'

'Yeah, I think she's really nice!' Della enthused. She'd never met anyone who was brave enough to hide in a bush and chuck olives at people before! But Della decided that it had actually been quite funny and that's definitely what she was looking forward to this holiday – fun!

Storm ambled along beside Della with his tail wagging and his pink tongue lolling out. There was a smudge of yellow pollen on his nose. Della smiled fondly at him, imagining the good time that she, Storm and Honey were going to have together.

Chapter
FIVE

'Can I go and call for Honey?' Della asked her mum the following day. 'I'm dying for a swim!'

'Maybe later, love. We're going shopping for food now.'

Della was about to protest when she remembered that she needed buy Storm some food with her pocket money. 'OK then,' she said, swallowing her impatience.

'I'll just get my shoulder bag.'

Storm ran upstairs with her. Della opened her bag and put it on the floor for Storm to get inside. 'I think you'll be safer in here,' she told him. 'Do you mind?'

'It is no problem!'

Della laughed as Storm took a flying leap, jumped straight in and curled up

next to her teddy-bear-shaped purse.

It was a short car ride to the nearest town. The big supermarket was on a side street and easy to find.

'I'll have to make sure they don't see me buying dog food,' Della whispered to Storm as her mum and dad began wheeling trolleys around. 'I'm going to get some . . . er, postcards and stuff,' she said in a louder voice, scooting off towards the pet-care section.

Once there, she grabbed a packet of dog food and immediately headed for the queue at the checkout.

A sudden thought struck her. 'Oh, no! I've only got English money,' she whispered. 'But I can't ask Mum or Dad to pay or they'll see what I'm buying. What am I going to do?'

'Do not worry. I will take care of it!' Storm woofed.

Della nodded. She couldn't see how Storm could solve her problem, but she trusted him so she stayed in the queue.

There were four people with loaded trolleys in front of them. Della chewed at her lip, fidgeting impatiently.

'I wish they'd hurry up. Mum and Dad are going to spot me at any moment,' she whispered.

She felt a faint prickling sensation flow down her spine and tiny gold sparks glinted in Storm's fluffy ginger-and-black fur. Suddenly there was a flash of light and an invisible wave of sparkles swept Della forward to the front of the queue. 'Oooh!' she exclaimed.

But no one seemed to have noticed

anything odd.

'*Hola.*' The smiling shop assistant
scanned the dog food.

'Um . . . *hola*,' Della answered nervously.
She reached into her bag and opened
her purse. Her eyes widened as she saw
that her English money had magically
transformed into euros!

She paid and slipped the bulky pack of
dog food into her bag, where it instantly
shrank to the size of a single bag of crisps.

'Wow! That was brilliant,' Della
whispered to Storm as she went back into
the shop.

Storm showed his teeth in a doggy
grin. 'I am glad I could help.'

They were only just in time. Della's
mum and dad were in a nearby aisle,
choosing breakfast cereal. They saw her
and waved.

'Pass your postcards over here, love. We
didn't get you any Spanish money yet, did
we?' her dad called.

'Oh . . . I . . . um, forgot that. Silly me!'
Della fibbed, walking towards them.

After the shopping had been dumped
in the car boot, Della, Storm and her

mum and dad wandered around the town square. Storm looped his front paws over the sides of the shoulder bag, craning his neck to peer at all the sights.

Trees cast shade over outside stalls. And a delicious smell wafted from where a man in a striped apron was cooking paella in a huge cast-iron pan.

Storm sniffed, his little button nose twitching, and licked his lips hungrily.

Della got the message. 'Can we try some of this, Dad?'

Mr Walton blinked at her. 'Really? Wouldn't you rather have pizza or chicken nuggets?'

'Da–ad! That's not all I eat,' Della said, nudging him playfully. 'I fancy trying something different.'

They sat at a wooden bench to eat bowls of the spicy rice, fish and vegetable mixture. Della sorted out a particularly large juicy prawn for Storm and put it on the bench beside her. He crunched it up with his little back teeth, his head on one side and one eye screwed shut in enjoyment.

Della's lips curved in a secret smile. She

loved having Storm for her friend.

When they got back to their villa an hour or so later, Honey was just walking up to their front drive. She had come to invite Della over for a swim. 'Mum and Dad said you're invited too,' she said, smiling at Della's parents.

'Yay! Let's go!' Della said eagerly, looking at her mum and dad. She was going to get a swim – at last!

'That sounds lovely,' Mrs Walton agreed. 'Thank you, Honey. Why don't you girls go ahead? We'll put the shopping away and follow you.'

Della could hardly wait. Dashing upstairs, she grabbed her swimming kit and then she, Storm and Honey strolled over to the Greens' villa.

A droning, buzzing sound, like someone running their nails across ridged cardboard, filled the hot air. 'That's the cicadas. They're like fat grasshoppers,' Honey said. 'They're harmless. In some parts of the world, people *eat* them! Can you believe it?'

'Yuck!' Della screwed up her face, impressed by Honey's knowledge.

At the villa, she quickly got changed. Honey's mum and dad were relaxing on sun loungers. They waved cheerily as the girls came out into the garden.

'Last one in eats a cicada burger!' yelled Honey as she raced towards the pool, hotly pursued by Della.

There was a huge splash as they both jumped in.

Storm sprawled on his side with his

pink tongue hanging out as he cooled
off in the shade while Honey and Della
messed about doing handstands in the
shallow end. After that they did some
lengths and then Della decided to float
about on her back for a while.

Honey had other ideas. She climbed
out, scrunched into a ball and dive-
bombed Della. 'Geronimo!'

A big wave slopped all over Della.

'You pest!' Della said, laughing. 'Don't
do that. I'm relaxing.'

'Tough!' Honey's eyes flashed with
mischief. She climbed out and dive-
bombed Della again.

This time Della kicked out strongly
and just managed to avoid being
swamped. 'Honey!'

Honey took no notice. She jumped in
time after time, splatting almost on top of
Della. After being bombed for about the
tenth time, Della's eyes were stinging. She
coughed, spitting out water.

'Hon-ey! Stop it! It's not funny any
more!' she spluttered, completely fed up
now.

Honey had surfaced, dripping, a big
grin on her face. 'I think it is!'

Della knew that her parents would have
stepped in and taken charge, but Honey's
mum and dad seemed to let Honey do

just what she liked. She gave up. Heaving herself out of the pool, she went over and spread her towel next to Storm.

The tiny puppy was dozing, his little paws flexing as he dreamed of chasing rabbits. He opened one sleepy blue eye and wagged his tail when Della threw herself on to her tummy.

'Aw! Come on back in. It was only a joke. Don't be such a wimp!' Honey jeered.

'In a little while,' Della said. 'Promise.'
She wanted Honey to think she was
having fun so they'd hang out together
again, but for now she needed a bit of a
break. Honey had so much energy!

Chapter
SIX

When Della woke the following morning, bars of sunlight were streaming in through the partially opened shutters.

Her mum and dad had decided to have a quiet day reading and relaxing by the pool. They suggested that Della might like to invite Honey over.

'Cool!' Della and Storm went to the Greens' villa straight after breakfast.

Honey was delighted. 'I've got a great idea!' she said, stopping dead as they were walking back up the hillside. 'Follow me!'

'Where are we going?' Della asked, a little wary after yesterday.

'You'll see,' Honey said, starting to jog in the opposite direction.

Della hung back and Storm paused invisibly beside her. 'I thought we were going back to my place. I ought to tell

Mum and Dad if we're going anywhere else. They're *really* strict about that.'

Honey rolled her eyes. 'Don't get into a major stress! Cripes! We'll only be gone for a few minutes.'

Della hesitated, but it was really hard to say no to Honey. She had a way of making her feel silly and fussy. 'Well – OK then. If we're quick,' she decided.

They set off again and soon came in sight of a familiar building. It was Maria Isola's farm.

'I'm not hiding in the garden and chucking things at people,' Della said, guessing that was what Honey had in mind.

'As if! Been there, done that,' Honey scoffed. 'I've got a much better idea.' She hared across the field and went into the grove of orange and lemon trees.

Della followed more slowly. She didn't feel quite right about being there.

'We're going to have a climbing contest!' Honey sang out. She grabbed a low branch and rapidly climbed upwards. Oranges fell out of the tree and bounced on to the grass. 'See, easy-peasy! Your

turn! Go on – climb that one,' Honey
urged, pointing.

Della stood there, undecided. Maybe
she should just go back to her villa,
but then Honey would think she was a
pathetic wimp.

Storm looked up at her. 'What do you
want to do?' he woofed.

'I guess I'll *have* to climb up,' Della
whispered to him.

Storm's furry brow wrinkled in a
frown. 'Are you good at climbing?'

'I've never tried. I don't like heights
much,' Della admitted.

'Come on then! What are you waiting
for?' Honey called.

Della swallowed hard. Reaching up,
she grasped a branch and felt around
for a foothold. Bracing herself against

the trunk, she heaved herself upwards.
Climbing was harder than she'd expected,
but with a lot of puffing and panting she
finally managed to scramble into the tree.

'Phew!' Della clung on tight, feeling
quite pleased with herself. Maybe Honey
was right and this was going to turn out
to be quite fun.

But when she looked down through
the branches at Storm, he seemed a long
way below her and looked even tinier
than usual. His bright-blue eyes were full
of concern.

Della started to feel dizzy and there was
a swirling feeling in her head.

Honey crowed with laughter from the
nearby tree. 'Gotcha! I never thought
you'd do it!' She climbed swiftly
downwards and jumped to the ground.

'See ya!' she called, racing back across the field and disappearing.

'Hey! Wait for . . . Oh, great,' Della groaned. Her heart sank as she realized that Honey had played a trick on her.

There was a movement from near the farmhouse. Someone began walking towards the trees.

Panicking, Della started to climb down, but in her hurry she missed her footing and her legs dangled in mid-air. She tried to hang on to a branch, but her fingers weren't strong enough and started slipping.

'Ooo-er!' Della gulped as her tummy lurched. She was going to fall!

Suddenly Della felt a warm tingling feeling down her spine, stronger than last time, as bright golden sparks ignited in

Storm's fluffy ginger-and-black fur and
tiny lightning bolts fizzed from his ears
and tail.

Della plunged downwards surrounded
by a silent whirlwind of golden sparks,
which swirled around her like tiny

worker bees. She tensed, ready for a jolt of pain, but instead of the bruising landing that she expected Della fell on to a deep pile of squishy green velvet cushions.

Plop! Plop! Plop! Oranges bounced down beside her, knocked off the branches by her fall.

A voice rang out as someone came closer. 'Della? Are you all right?' Maria's face was creased with concern.

Della felt the velvet cushions disappear one by one and she sat there on the grass unable to believe that she hadn't hurt herself.

Storm ran up, jumped into her lap and started licking her face. 'Thanks, Storm,' she whispered, moving him gently aside as she struggled to her feet. 'I'm OK!' she said in a louder voice so that Maria could hear her.

'I am glad. You can help yourself to oranges whenever you like,' Maria said gently. 'But maybe you should ask Carmella to help you pick them.'

'I wasn't picking ora– I was . . . We were . . . I mean . . .' Della stammered and then fell silent. She was furious with Honey but she wasn't prepared to snitch on her, even if it would get her out of trouble. 'I'm really sorry,' she finished miserably.

'I accept your apology. Let us say no more about it,' Maria said, patting her arm. 'Are you sure that you were alone just now?'

Della nodded, mutely, her face burning.

'Very well. I do not think I need to tell

your parents about this,' Maria said kindly. 'Off you go, Della.'

Storm trotted alongside her as she walked quickly across the field without turning back. She felt awful about fibbing to Maria, but she didn't think she had much choice.

Honey was waiting for her a bit further on. 'You took your time. What happened?'

'Maria thought I was pinching oranges. She said I could have as many as I like. I only had to ask.'

'That's hilarious!' Honey clapped her hands to her mouth and burst out laughing.

Della didn't think it was funny and was still too annoyed about Honey's mean trick to talk to her just then. She marched up the hillside towards her villa with

Storm, leaving Honey to follow her.

'It was just only a joke! You didn't get much of a telling-off, did you?' Honey called after her. 'Look, I'm sorry, Della. Let's still be friends?'

Della sighed and stopped, waiting for Honey to catch up. She guessed that, even with Storm keeping her company, the holiday was definitely more interesting with Honey around.

Honey looked at Della solemnly. 'I'm glad you got down the tree safely. Otherwise you'd be orange squash!'

The two girls burst into giggles and carried on back up the hill together.

Chapter
SEVEN

The following day the two families had planned a shared trip to the seaside. Della was really looking forward to it. She had decided to forget about yesterday and hoped Honey wasn't in too much of a joke-playing mood.

She began putting some last-minute things into her shoulder bag. 'Swimming costume, towel, dog food for Storm,' she said, mentally ticking things off. 'Oh, where are my other flip-flops?'

'I will find them,' Storm woofed helpfully, diving into the bottom of her wardrobe and emerging with a flip-flop dangling from his mouth.

'Thanks, Storm.' Della smiled at him as she took the now slightly damp shoe and then reached in for the other one. Her fingers closed on something big and leggy.

'Aaargh!' Della shrieked, shooting backwards and sitting down hard on her behind.

'Yipe!' Taken by surprise, Storm almost jumped out of his fur.

He leapt into the wardrobe again and came out carrying the most enormous plastic spider Della had ever seen. Shaking his head and growling, he tossed it across the room.

'It's OK. It's not real,' Della spluttered, laughing now that her heartbeat had returned to normal. 'Honey must have sneaked up here yesterday and put it there. It *was* pretty funny. I don't mind jokes like that. I bet they heard me screaming in England!' She shook her head slowly as she finished packing her bag.

'The Greens are here. Are you ready, Della?' Mr Walton called up the stairs.

'Coming!' Della and Storm ran down, went outside and piled into the back of the Greens' people carrier. Honey was already in the back. Della plonked down next to her.

'Thanks for the *pet* spider! It was a bit *small*. Couldn't you find a bigger, blacker, hairier one?' she joked.

'What spider?' Honey tried to look innocent but she couldn't help grinning. 'I couldn't resist it. Glad you liked it. I've brought my new kite with me,' she said, changing the subject. 'I hope it's windy enough to fly it. We can take turns with it.'

'Sounds great. Thanks, Honey,' she said, touched by the other girl's generosity.

This was the Honey she really liked and wanted to be friends with.

She sat stroking Storm, who was on the seat beside her, nearest the car door. After a while he stood up on his little back legs to look out of the window, his ears flapping in the breeze.

They reached the coast twenty minutes later. Mrs Green parked the car and they all walked the few metres to a wide beach with pale, silvery sand. Creamy-topped waves were gently rolling in and breaking on the shore.

It was very hot, but there was a strong breeze blowing.

'Perfect for kite-flying later,' Honey announced.

Storm's nose twitched as he smelled the salty air. His little paws kicked up spurts of sand as he scampered invisibly after Della.

The mums set up a striped windbreak and the dads went off to buy everyone ice creams. While they were waiting for them to return, Honey and Della made a sandcastle.

The castle of heaped sand was soon patted into shape, but it was a bit lumpy. Honey thought it was in need of a tower or two, but they hadn't any buckets with them to make some.

'At least we can make a moat,' Della said. Storm came and stood very close to her hands, so he could enjoy digging too without Honey noticing. His little paws pedalled like fury and he yapped with enjoyment as sand flew everywhere.

'Wow! You work fast!' Honey said, impressed, as Della appeared to have dug a moat in double-quick time.

'Yeah, don't I just!' Della replied, grinning.

The dads arrived with ice creams. Della and Honey sat on the sand to eat theirs. Della sneaked a fingerful of ice cream to

Storm when no one was looking.

Honey finished hers first. She
looked sideways at Della and a familiar
mischievous expression crossed her face.
Reaching out, Honey snatched her half-
finished ice cream.

'Hey!' Della cried.

She watched in disbelief as Honey
leapt to her feet and dumped the half-
eaten cone upside down on top of their

sandcastle. 'Perfect. One pointed tower!'

'Why didn't you use your own cone? I was enjoying that!' Della grumbled.

'Haha! I'll buy you another one,' Honey laughed.

'Don't bother!' Della stomped down to the shore, where she paddled about by herself in the cool water. 'Honey just can't help herself! She makes me so mad!'

Storm was nodding sympathetically when he was almost drenched by an incoming wave. Barking crossly at the sea, he dodged backwards to keep from getting his paws wet.

Della felt her mood lifting as she laughed at his antics. Storm always seemed to find a way to cheer her up, even when he didn't mean to!

'Della! Do you want a go with my

kite?' Honey yelled, waving.

Della looked up the beach. She shrugged. 'Might as well. No sense in holding a grudge. Come on, Storm,' she called softly.

When Della reached her, Honey held out the kite and a long length of string, but she kept hold of the reel with the rest of the string wrapped round it. The kite was shaped like a blue-and-orange butterfly and had two long flowing tails.

Della reached out and took hold of the butterfly wings.

'I will hold it for you!' Storm woofed helpfully. He grabbed one of the kite's long tails in his teeth.

'No, don't! It could be dangerous . . .' Della cautioned, realizing that Storm probably hadn't seen a kite before and didn't know how it worked.

It was too late. 'OK. Go!' Honey ordered, and pulled down hard on the kite strings just as it billowed in a gust of wind, deliberately jerking it out of Della's hands. The orange-and-blue butterfly flapped as it began to rise, with Storm still dangling from its long tail.

Chapter
EIGHT

Storm gave a muffled whine of alarm as
he hung from the kite tail.

'Hey! Where did that puppy come
from?' Honey shouted.

Della realized that Storm was so
scared that he must have forgotten to be
invisible. She didn't think twice.

One step. Two Steps. Three steps. She
leapt high into the air. Yes! Della just

managed to grab hold of Storm round his middle. 'I've got you!'

The tiny puppy let go of the kite, which zoomed straight up into the air until it was flying many metres above them.

Della landed awkwardly and twisted her ankle. 'Oh!' she gasped as a sharp pain took her breath away. She lay on her side on the sand, holding the shocked puppy.

Across the beach, Honey was rooted to the spot with her mouth hanging open.

'Thank you for saving me, Della,' Storm woofed.

'I'm just glad you're all right. I couldn't
bear anything to happen to you.' She
winced. Her entire leg seemed to be
aching and she couldn't move.

Storm's midnight-blue eyes widened.
'You are hurt. I will make you better.'

Della felt a familiar tingling down
her spine as Storm once again became
invisible. He then opened his mouth and
huffed out a cloud of tiny gold sparks
as fine as gold dust. The glittering mist
swirled round Della's leg. The pain in her
ankle felt very hot for a second and then
it turned ice cold and completely drained
away as if it was being carried out to sea
by the tide.

'Thanks, Storm. I'm fine now,' Della
said. She rolled over and got to her feet,
just as Honey thrust the kite-reel at a

nearby boy and ran up to her.

'Oh, my gosh! What happened? Where's that puppy gone? Have you hurt yourself?' she asked, white-faced.

Della took a deep breath. She could just about cope with Honey's annoying tricks and teasing ways, but it was a different matter when they put Storm in danger.

'I don't know where the puppy went. It ran away. But I've really had it with you! What kind of cruel person gets their laughs from making someone else feel angry and upset?' she fumed. 'I'm not hurt, but I could have been. You're such a muppet! You never think about anyone but yourself!'

'I . . . I . . .' Honey opened and closed her mouth. Two bright spots of colour

glowed on her cheeks. She looked
shocked and had obviously never thought
about it like that.

Della didn't wait for a reply. She walked
past Honey, stormed up the beach and
threw herself down on the sand. She
needed time to calm down.

Storm followed her. He laid his chin on her knee and looked at her with big solemn eyes. 'I do not think that Honey is a bad person.'

'Me neither. I do like her. If only she'd stop being such a pest. I really don't think Honey understands how rotten it feels to have jokes played on you all the time.' She stroked Storm's fluffy sun-warmed fur sadly. 'Well, I've done it now. Honey will probably never speak to me again. Thank goodness I've got you. You're a proper friend. I hope you'll live with me for always.'

A serious expression crossed Storm's pointed little face. 'That is not possible. I must return to my home world one day, to fight Shadow and force him to leave our lands. I will become leader of the

Moon-claw pack. Do you understand that, Della?'

Della nodded. She felt a pang as she didn't think she'd ever be ready to lose her amazing puppy friend. 'But that won't be for a long time, will it?' she asked.

'I do not know, but I will stay as long as I can,' Storm woofed softly.

'That's OK then.' Della forced all thoughts of his leaving out of her mind. She decided that she was going to enjoy every single moment she could with Storm. She jumped up and ran across the sand. 'Come on, let's go exploring for shells!'

Della didn't see Honey the following day. She was starting to feel a bit bad about having a go at her, even though Honey

had unknowingly put Storm in danger.
But it was too late to take back what
she'd said.

Della decided to spend the day lazing
by the pool with Storm instead. Her
mum came up to where she was lying on
a sun lounger, reading under an umbrella.

'Aren't you going to call for Honey?'
she asked.

Della shook her head.

Mrs Walton looked thoughtful. 'Have
you two fallen out or something?'

'Not exactly,' Della said evasively.
'Maybe I'll see her later.' *Or she might
call for me*, she found herself thinking
hopefully.

The day after and there was still no sign
of Honey, so that afternoon Della and
Storm visited a medieval hill-town with

her mum and dad.

There was a fiesta, celebrating the birthday of its patron saint. The tall buildings of sand-coloured stone were strewn with flags and ribbons and a band led a colourful parade.

A large splashing stone fountain helped cool the hot air. Della and Storm nibbled at some *churros*, long thin doughnuts, as they watched the people in costumes holding up a picture of a woman in long robes, decorated with flowers.

'I bet Honey would have loved this,' Della said wistfully.

Storm nodded.

It was late when they got back and Della went straight up to bed. 'Sweet dreams,' she said, cuddling Storm in the darkness.

*

A loud growling and snapping sound from outside woke her an hour later. Della shot upright and switched on her bedside lamp.

She reached out to see if Storm was awake, but he wasn't on the bed. 'Storm?' she whispered.

There was no answer. Where could he be?

Chapter
NINE

Della heard a tiny whine of terror. It was coming from under the bed.

She jumped out and bent down to look beneath it. Storm was curled into a tiny ball, pressed up against the wall. She saw that the little puppy was trembling.

'What's wrong? Are you sick?' she asked worriedly.

'I sense that Shadow knows where I

am. I heard those dogs outside and I think he has set them on to me,' he whimpered.

Della felt a stir of alarm, but the barking and growling was already beginning to fade and soon silence fell, except for the odd buzz of the cicadas. She went over to the window and opened the shutters a crack so that she could peep out.

'There aren't any there now. Maybe it was just the farm dogs,' she told him. 'How will I know they're Shadow's dogs, if he does send any?'

Storm lifted his head. 'They will be ordinary dogs, with fierce pale eyes and extra-long sharp teeth. Shadow's magic will make any dog I meet into my enemy now.'

'Then I'll have to make extra sure

that you keep well hidden,' Della said.
She reached right under the bed with
one hand and stroked Storm with gentle
fingertips.

The terrified puppy slowly uncurled.
He crawled towards her with his ears
flattened and little tummy pressed to the
ground.

Della gently picked him up and got
back into bed with him. She could feel
his heart beating rapidly against her
fingers.

'You're safe now,' she crooned. 'I hope that horrible Shadow will keep on going and never be seen again!'

Storm twisted round to look up at her, his little pointed face serious. 'He will never stop looking for me. If he comes back I may have to leave suddenly, without saying goodbye.'

Della nodded sadly as she was reminded again that she couldn't keep Storm with her forever. She kissed the top of his soft little head and rubbed her chin in his fur, sure that she wouldn't sleep a wink now.

But seconds later she was fast asleep.

'*Hola!*' Carmella called at the kitchen door, her arms full of clean towels. 'How are you?'

Della was helping herself to orange juice from the fridge. She looked up and smiled at the Spanish girl. 'Hi! I'm fine, thanks.'

Carmella smiled back. She came inside and had a word with Della's mum, who was in the sitting room writing postcards.

After a few minutes Carmella reappeared with the laundry. She paused on her way out to speak to Della. 'See you tonight for the barbecue at the farm! You are all invited.'

'Great. See you there,' Della said. She turned to Storm when Carmella had gone. 'Sounds like fun!' she whispered and she had a thought. 'I wonder if Honey will be there.'

Storm looked up at her with his sparkling blue eyes. 'I hope so. That would be fun.' There had been no more signs of any fierce dogs and Storm seemed back to his usual self.

Della wondered what would happen if she and Honey met up again. It was three days since the beach trip. Would Honey be glad to see her? Or would she just ignore her?

'Maybe I should go round to the villa and talk to her. Or I could write a note and slip it through the door,' Della said to Storm. 'I can't decide what to do. What do you think?'

Storm put his head on one side. 'What do you want to do?' he woofed.

Della was silent for a moment. 'I want to be friends with her again,' she said finally. It was true, she realized. She missed Honey. 'I know. I'll buy her a present. I can give it to her at the barbecue.'

Storm nodded. 'I think Honey would like that.'

Della went to find her mum to ask if they could drive into town. Mrs Walton agreed readily. 'I want to get some stamps and post these cards anyway.'

Della and Storm went into a shop with her. There was a display of soft

toys and Della immediately pounced on
a gorgeous, realistic-looking Labrador
puppy. It had plushy cream fur and
melting brown eyes.

'Any girl would love this,' she said,
reaching for her teddy-bear purse.

Storm nodded agreement.

'What a cute toy. I didn't know that
you were into puppies in a big way,' her
mum commented as they returned to the
car.

'Oh, I am – hugely!' Della said,
grinning. If only her mum knew! 'But it's
not for me. It's for Honey.'

'Ah. I see,' her mum said, sounding as if
she understood completely.

Della could hardly wait for the evening.
As soon as it was dark they all strolled
down the hillside to Maria's farm.

Guitar music floated towards them.
Strings of coloured lights glowed from
the trees and a delicious smell rose from
the barbecue, where meat was sizzling.
Maria, her husband and Carmella
welcomed them. Farm workers stood
around chatting and smiling in a friendly
manner.

Della looked around for Honey, but the
Green family hadn't arrived yet. 'I hope
Honey's coming,' Della whispered to
Storm, looking at the toy Labrador.

There was no reply.

With a whine of terror, Storm raced
towards the grove of orange and lemon
trees.

Della whipped round and saw two
small dogs running into the courtyard.
They raised their heads and she saw their

abnormally long teeth and fierce pale eyes. Her heart missed a beat. They were here for Storm!

Her friend was in terrible danger. Della dashed towards the trees and reached them just as there was a bright golden flash. She blinked as her sight cleared. Storm stood there as his real wolf self. His dazzling silver-grey fur gleamed with bright sparks and his midnight-blue eyes glowed like jewels. A she-wolf with a gentle face and kind eyes stood next to Storm.

And then Della knew that Storm was leaving for good.

A sob rose in her throat, but she forced herself to be brave for her friend's sake. 'Your enemies are close. Save yourself, Storm!'

Storm raised a large silver paw in farewell. 'You have been a good friend. Thank you for helping me, Della,' he said in a deep velvety growl.

There was an ache in Della's chest and her eyes stung with tears. She was going to miss Storm terribly. 'Goodbye. Take care. I'll never forget you,' she whispered hoarsely.

There was a final bright flash and a silent explosion of sparks that sprinkled harmlessly around her like glittering sand.

Storm and his mother faded and then disappeared. The dogs ran through the trees. Della saw their teeth and eyes instantly return to normal before they turned and slunk away.

Della blinked away tears as she went slowly back towards the farmhouse. At least she'd had a chance to say goodbye to Storm. She knew she'd never forget the wonderful adventure she'd shared with the magic puppy.

'I know you'll be a wonderful leader some day. The Moon-claw pack is lucky to have you,' she said breathlessly.

A figure ran towards her. 'There you are! This is for you,' Honey said. She held out a toy puppy with fluffy ginger-and-black fur. 'It reminded me of that puppy on the beach.'

'I absolutely love it!' Della said, gathering the toy into her arms. 'I bought something for you too.' She gave Honey the Labrador puppy.

'Wow! Thanks. It's adorable!' Honey gave a shaky smile. 'So – does this mean we're friends again? I'm so sorry, Della.'

'Definitely friends again. But no more silly pranks. OK?' She remembered the plastic spider in her wardrobe. 'This isn't a trick puppy, is it?'

'Not exactly!' Honey showed Della the secret pocket, like a tiny furry pouch, which had a small card inside. On it was

printed. '*I am your special friend. My name is
. . .*' There was a gap to write the name of
your choice.

'No contest. I know exactly what I'm
going to call my puppy!' Della said, her
heart lifting, as she linked arms with
Honey.

Magic Ponies

Could you be a little pony's special friend?

Could you be a little pony's special friend?

Magic Ponies
A New Friend

SUE BENTLEY

Could you be a little pony's special friend?

Magic Ponies
A Special Wish

SUE BENTLEY

Out Now

A little puppy, a sprinkling of magic, a forever friend . . .

Magic Puppy

Sparkling Skates

SUE BENTLEY

puffin.co.uk

Coming Soon

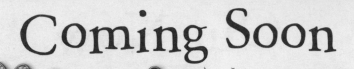

Magic Puppy

Spellbound at School   The Perfect Secret

Magic Puppy

A New Beginning
9780141323503

Muddy Paws
9780141323510

Cloud Capers
9780141323527

Star of the Show
9780141323534

Party Dreams
9780141323794

A Forest Charm
9780141323800

Twirling Tails
9780141323817

School of Mischief
9780141323824

Snowy Wishes
9780141323831

Classroom Princess
9780141324791

Friendship Forever
9780141324784

Sparkling Skates
9780141324777

Sunshine Shimmers
9780141324760

Spellbound at School
9780141324753

Coming Soon

The Perfect Secret
9780141324746

A little puppy
a sprinkling of magic,
a forever friend

puffin.co.uk

If you like Magic Puppy, you'll love **Magic Kitten**

A Summer Spell
9780141320144

Classroom Chaos
9780141320151

Star Dreams
9780141320168

Double Trouble
9780141320175

Moonlight Mischief
9780141321530

A Circus Wish
9780141321547

Sparkling Steps
9780141321554

A Glittering Gallop
9780141321561

Seaside Mystery
9780141321981

Firelight Friends
9780141321998

A Shimmering Splash
9780141322001

A Puzzle of Paws
9780141322018

A Christmas Surprise
9780141323237

Picture Perfect
9780141323480

A Splash of Forever
9780141323497

OUT NOW

Full of grrreat stickers and activities

A **purrfect** recipe for fun!

Magic Puppy

Win a Magic Puppy goody bag!

The evil wolf Shadow has ripped out part of Storm's
letter from his mother and hidden the words so that magic puppy
Storm can't find them.

Storm needs your help!

Two words have been hidden in secret bones in *Sunshine Shimmers*.
Find the hidden words and put them
together to complete the message from Storm's mother.
Send it in to us and each month we will put every correct message
in a draw and pick out one lucky winner, who will receive
a Magic Puppy gift – definitely worth barking about!

Send the hidden message, your name and address on a postcard to:
Magic Puppy Competition
Puffin Books
80 Strand
London WC2R 0RL
Good luck!

puffin.co.uk

It all started with a Scarecrow

Puffin is well over sixty years old.
Sounds ancient, doesn't it? But Puffin has never been
so lively. We're always on the lookout for the next big
idea, which is how it began all those years ago.

Penguin Books was a big idea from the mind of
a man called Allen Lane, who in 1935 invented
the quality paperback and changed the world.
**And from great Penguins, great Puffins grew,
changing the face of children's books forever.**

The first four Puffin Picture Books were hatched in 1940 and the
first Puffin story book featured a man with broomstick arms called
Worzel Gummidge. In 1967 Kaye Webb, Puffin Editor, started the
Puffin Club, promising to **'make children into readers'**.
She kept that promise and over 200,000 children became
devoted Puffineers through their quarterly installments of
Puffin Post, which is now back for a new generation.

Many years from now, we hope you'll look back and
remember Puffin with a smile. **No matter what your age
or what you're into, there's a Puffin for everyone.**
The possibilities are endless, but one thing is for sure:
whether it's a picture book or a paperback, a sticker book
or a hardback, **if it's got that little Puffin
on it – it's bound to be good.**